Dance Me, Daddy

Written by award-winning
singer and songwriter

Cindy Morgan

illustrated by

Philomena O'Neill

 ZONDERkidz

Spinning around on the tops of his feet, she smiles like an angel and looks up so sweet. She wears a princess gown and a cardboard crown, and her piggy tails dance and swirl. He's her hero, brave and strong, and she's her daddy's girl.

He tells her jokes and makes her laugh. They
play I spy, let's pretend, and catch me if you can.

When the moon is out and the sun is asleep,
    after dinner, dessert, and bedtime stories,
        she climbs up on the tops of his feet and says . . .

"Dance me, Daddy. Dance me around.
Don't let my feet ever touch down.
There's nothing better than being your girl.
If I am your princess, then you are king of the world."

Days turn to years, and his little girl grows.
She packs away princess gowns and crowns and bows.
She meets new friends and wears different clothes.

Sometimes when she's sleeping, he kneels by her bed to pray that her Father in heaven is watching over her every moment of every day.

Even though some things change,
some things stay the same.

When the moon is out and the sun is asleep, after dinner, homework, and a little TV, they turn up the music and in his arms she swings.

"Dance me, Daddy. Dance me around.
Don't let my feet ever touch down.
There's nothing better than being your girl.
If I am your princess, then you are king of the world."

One day her daddy waves good-bye. He always knew this day would come, when his little girl would be all grown up, when she'd go off to see the world, meet a boy, and fall in love.

Her wedding day arrives, and the church bells chime.
In her white princess gown she smiles that same smile.

And even though some things change,
some things stay the same.

By the light of the moon and that same sweet song,
she steps into her daddy's arms before the moment is gone.